THE HOUSE OF UNTOLD STORIES

pocket-sized fables & fictions

PETER CHIYKOWSKI

Andrews McMeel
PUBLISHING®

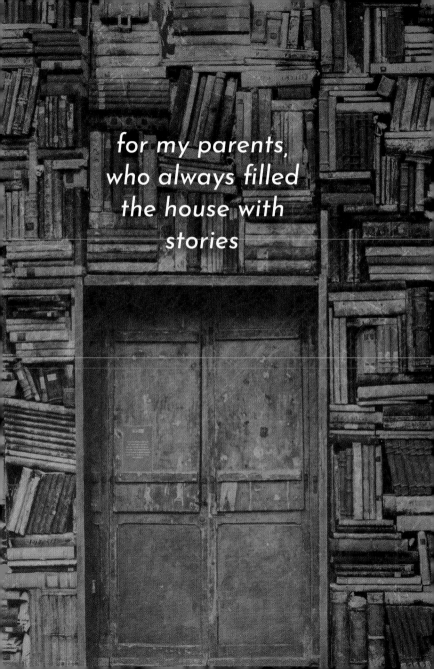

for my parents,
who always filled
the house with
stories

THE HOUSE OF UNTOLD STORIES

One day you are walking down a street you know well, and you see the House where nothing should be, standing across an overgrown field behind a drooping chain-link fence. Your curiosity gets the better of you. You approach, and the House seems so familiar, the way a stranger in a dream feels like an old friend you haven't thought about in years.

You wander in to find that the House is not so much a house as a convergence of places half-remembered, half-forgotten, or fully imagined. The dust motes dancing in the slanted sunlight of the hall remind you of the empty foyer of your childhood home the day your family moved out. The oaky musk of polished wood and yellowed paper reaches deep into the crowded cupboard of your mind, as if rummaging for a memory at the very back of your awareness, or perhaps trying to plant one there.

The House is impossible . . . Its doors lead to stories, confessions, dreams, prayers, and worlds that never quite were. The hall closet opens to an apartment complex at the end of days. The pantry leads to a bunker on a planet humans will never discover. The walkway to the courtyard passes through the fantasy kingdom you imagined your bedroom to be when you were a child.

Some say the House is an orphanage for fantasies we outgrow. Or a runaway colony for stories we meant to write. A labyrinth to contain nightmares we wish to forget and the dreams that give us too much hope to bear. A seed vault for myths in long hibernation.

Whatever it is, there's a reason the House called you here. Somewhere in its halls, a story is waiting for you. And whether you pluck it like a flower and knowingly carry it from the House, or whether the motion of your passing causes it to burst like a dandelion halo and scatter its seeds in the tangle of your mind, that story has chosen you as its bearer.

So please, stay as long as you like. Wander long and free. Leave when you're ready. But do not be surprised if the next time you return, one of the stories has moved on, and in its place a new story is sprouting, waiting for you to carry it out into the world.

LIGHTHOUSES

The young ones never believe me when I tell them what lighthouses were in the days before.

They have never lived in a world where rain falls from the sky clean and drinkable. Where warm sunlight strokes your skin without tangling its mutating fingers in your DNA. Where ships sail across an ocean teeming with life, and not boiling with acid and the rage of a shattered planet.

They have no concept of a time where lighthouses steered ships away from land.

In the ruins of the world, they only know the beacons by their new meaning.

A warning.

Stay away from the water.

LOST BASILISK

I used to put up fake "lost pet" posters for mythical creatures, just to keep my neighborhood interesting.
    "LOST BASILISK: ANSWERS TO BALTHAZAR."
    "MISSING CHUPACABRA: $500 REWARD!"
    "ESCAPED GRIFFIN: CALL THIS NUMBER!"

Somebody just responded to my ad about the runaway phoenix, and now they're on their way here with a reinforced steel cargo container that's already starting to melt.

It might be time to move.

WITCHES' DEEP

They told her it was daft to build a castle in a swamp, let alone Witches' Deep, but she seemed determined. The land hadn't been used in years, and the mayor was happy to sell it cheap to this outsider who didn't know its secrets: that the water swam with restless souls. That the townsfolk had used it to drown their witches, bound and weighed with large stones around their necks, during the purges. That the pitiful creatures had made a last stand together, mustering under a sackcloth banner of a waxing moon and pleading to be left alone to carry out their studies in peace. The townsfolk overpowered them and threw them into the depths all the same.

But all this they kept to themselves.

And so up the woman's castle went—a proud stronghold of shining limestone. It had tall towers and long, sprawling hallways filled with vast libraries, workshops, and laboratories. Dark, round rocks dotted its bright walls.

And then down the castle went, sinking into the hungry muck the very next day.

"Why build yourself a castle only to see it fall?" the mayor asked the woman as the townsfolk gathered to watch the spectacle. Only a single parapet remained visible above the dark waters. The woman hadn't even had time to hang a banner.

"Oh," said the woman, smiling. "I didn't build it for myself."

And then came a sound from the depths. A winch turning. And onto the parapet rose the damp sackcloth banner of a waxing moon.

"I made it for them."

The mayor thought of the dark stones he had seen dotting the castle walls. He thought of the weights he had tied around the necks of witches, darker now after so many years at the bottom of Witches' Deep.

And as the first of the unburdened witches climbed from the murk to gather on the sunken parapet, dripping with mud and malice, he wondered if it was too late to apologize.

THE GODS
MEET

"I am the god Vulcan, and humanity will keep the flame of my memory alive in the fires of the burning volcano."

The gods nodded in approval.

"I am the goddess Ceres, and the humans will grow my memory anew each season in the harvest of their grains and cereals."

"It is good to be remembered," the gods agreed.

"I am the god Pluto, and humanity will look to the heavens and forever remember me for my greatest namesake: a planet of my own."

"Actually . . ." said the other gods. "We heard they're demoting you to planetoid."

"Fine," said Pluto, "I guess I'll be the god of killing everyone."

For centuries, our cult has called on Yoggoroth the Devouring One to solve our problems. Recite the right incantation through a portal to the Evervoid, tell Yoggoroth what you need, and infinite cosmic power is yours to wield.

When a rival attacked our sanctum, we recited the Ritual of Fangs.

LET YOUR ENEMIES DROWN IN BLOOD, they replied in a voice like exploding rainbow static.

When a new recruit got in trouble with the law, we recited the Ritual of Obliteration.

IT SHALL BE FORGOTTEN.

When the cult needed money for a new regional chapter, we recited the Ritual of Riches.

SURE, SURE, BUG ME INSTEAD OF APPLYING FOR A LOAN.

Over time, Yoggoroth responded less and less. We were puzzled. We had followed the rituals word for word! But then again, perhaps that was the problem.

One night we recited the Ritual of Inquisition, which allows us to pose a single question and receive an answer borne of eldritch insight.

"How are you doing?" we asked.

A pause. Then a choked sob, echoing through infinity. *NO ONE HAS EVER ASKED ME THAT. PEOPLE START ALL THESE CULTS TO WORSHIP YOU, BUT THEY NEVER ASK YOU IF YOU WANT WORSHIP. SOMETIMES YOU JUST NEED SOMEONE TO TALK TO.*

We spoke for hours. When we were done, we ended the ritual, saying, "Let's talk again soon." We meant it.

Now we do weekly check-ins. We ask questions and listen. We call them "Yog," which they prefer. We still request help sometimes, but we don't assume it.

We have new incantation: the Ritual of "How Are You Doing, Old Friend?"

It might just be the most powerful one yet.

AFTER THE SUNSET

The newly minted couple drove off into the sunset, leaving all the problems of their old life in the rearview mirror. The sun took them in, and they sped along a highway of golden light, solar flares blooming like cacti on their left, sunspots yawning like desert craters on their right. After a while, the bright light made their eyes water and their heads ache. Truth be told, the terrain was somewhat monotonous.

"What now?" he asked.

"I don't know," she replied.

They found a sun-motel for the night. There was an awkward moment when they hesitated over who would pay.

"I haven't canceled my rent checks yet," she said. "And tomorrow's the first."

"I'm already at my credit limit for the month," he said. "And I don't know the exchange rate here."

They split the cost two ways, and neither felt like they got what they paid for. The bed was saggy, the headboard creaked, and the television only had local sun channels. They had no context for any of the celebrities or political jokes.

The next morning, over rubbery sunny-side up eggs and watered-down tequila sunrises, they agreed this wasn't working. Instead, they would try driving off into the sunrise to see if that was any better, perhaps stopping over to check on their old lives with new eyes first.

Returning wouldn't solve any of their problems, but neither had running, and at least the coffee was decent in the real world.

THE MUSIC BOX: PART I

My mother once told me that love is like a haunted music box you find in the basement and almost open to unwittingly unleash an army of one thousand anguished spirits on the world.

"That's oddly specific. What do you mean?" I asked her.

She sighed. "You'll understand when you're older."

The rune-etched chains across the cellar door rattled ominously.

THE GLITCH

My heart sinks in my chest as you steer our chopper toward the mountain. The Glitch—or whatever HQ calls the spatial anomaly eddying around the mountain—shimmers. We check our instruments. Our position jumps again, sending us back over the same half mile of tundra.

HQ should have given us more intel. It was only when we spotted the other crashed chopper that we realized they'd lied about us being the first team sent in. You and I agree not to report back until we know why. You lower our flight path into the cover of a frozen trench when the commlink crackles to life with static and panic.

"Kkkkkk—Expedition Team Alpha—kkkkkk—urn back—"

Another chopper comes out of nowhere, rear rotor damaged and cockpit full of smoke. You swerve right, catching the canyon wall with our tail. The impact showers the chopper with ice and rock. I smell fumes.

"Bail out?" you ask, hand trembling on the stick.

"Set us down. We'll assess damage first."

You maneuver out of the trench. As you touch down up top, the skids cause the plateau to crumble away, exposing another chopper buried in snow. My heart stops when I make out the pilots. It's us, half-frozen and barely conscious.

I don't have to give the order for you to pull up and turn us back. The engine coughs with blowback. You speed toward HQ as our vision clouds with black fumes, and I can barely make out another chopper headed for the mountain. It ducks down toward the trench. I grab the radio to hail them.

"This is Expedition Team Alpha! Turn back! Turn back!"

And suddenly we warp position again, dropping into their flight path. Eyes stinging with smoke, I see my own panicked face in the incoming cockpit as the chopper swerves into the wall. You turn us back after them, but the engine sputters out. It's all you can do to set us down with a crunch in deep snow. Outside, the wind howls, burying us deeper.

I know with a dread certainty that somewhere in the blinding white outside, we are just now setting out from HQ to explore the anomaly. Somewhere we are spotting a crashed chopper and deciding not to call it in. We are hearing a Mayday call and swerving to avoid an incoming chopper.

And it's just a matter of time until touch down to find ourselves here, half-dead in the snow. And we will do nothing to help. Because somehow, I already know none of us are getting off this mountain alive.

EXORCIZE
REGIME

There's an awkward moment when people find out my job is exercising demons.

"Oh, like 'The power of Christ compels you!?'"

I understand the confusion. Most of us don't realize that demons are destructive for the same reasons as the rest of us: they're frustrated or anxious or sad or they've just had a rough go of things lately. They feel trapped in their own lives and want to hop into somebody else's. We've all been there. Has being shouted at ever helped?

Probably not.

That's why I exercise demons. Morning yoga classes. A game of pick-up football at lunch. Cooperative games at night, followed by a debrief. A little workout for heart, mind, and body. *What did we learn? How's everyone doing? Do you need someone to talk to?* It doesn't solve their issues, but it helps them develop new ways to manage, and that's a start. They've felt the wrong kind of burn for too long.

"The power of yoga compels you!" doesn't sound as badass, but sweat is easier to come by than holy water, and there's nothing better to help you leave your body behind—even just for a few minutes.

THE
HOMONYM
WIZARD

People didn't understand the power of the homonym wizard. So what if he could turn a bat into a bat or a bark into bark?

The homonym wizard didn't mind. When people were mean to him, he assumed *mean* was average. When they were *kind*, he treated them of a similar type.

"You magic is useless. How do you *stand* it?" they asked him.

"I don't take it lying down," he replied.

"Does it make you *cross*?"

"Only the street."

"All your incantations sound the same," they complained.

"Ah," he said, "just wait until you see how I spell them."

THREE MONTHS TO LIVE

My doctor gave me three months to live.
    My old dentist gave me two.
    My neighbor only gave me a few weeks.

If I'm going to keep hacking it as a vampire, I need to find more nutritious meals.

WHEN THE LIFEBOATS LEFT

When the lifeboats left in search of a planet that was not dying, only the rich could afford seats. They transferred all their credits into interstellar accounts and blasted off for a new life amongst the stars while the rest of us working schlubs were sealed inside the coffin Earth had become.

We started to shut down our factories and vehicles, planning to conserve the supplies, fuel, and atmosphere we had left. We ate lightly, lived simply, and savored the days.

Because we were already accustomed to making do with less, it was easier than we thought. Over time, the air began to clear, and the sounds of life returned to our wetlands. Without the voices of the powerful urging us to buy, sell, work, live as fast as we can, we found new rhythms.

Today, Earth is much how it was centuries ago, although we've managed to maintain the most important scientific breakthroughs: medical knowledge, communication technology, infrastructure.

We just restored an old interstellar communicator, and we've been debating telling the lifeboats that it's safe to come back now. Some of us think they caused the problems in the first place, while others contend that we all had a hand in it.

The one thing we all agree on is this: it's never too late to turn the ship around.

THE
CANDIDATES

The year 3020 had one of the most contentious presidential debates in history.

Slaughterbot of the Robot Party said he was pro killing all humans.

Bob of the Human Party said he was against it.

The next day, the papers called it a toss-up.

The headline ran: "Human Party Refuses to Compromise."

Tired of the sound of my voice, of the messes I made whenever I opened my mouth, I drove to the quarry outside of town. I shouted all of my frustration into the rocky walls. Then, like an owner abandoning their dog, I ran back to my car and drove off before my voice could fetch my echo back to me. I was too ashamed to even cock an ear back down the dusty road.

At first my echo dogged me like a stray. I could hear it bounce around the neighborhood, resonating in the hulls of dumpsters and reverberating down alleys looking for me. I couldn't bear the thought of hearing myself again, of my clumsy voice bounding in the doorway and causing a scene. So I moved across the country. I made new friends. They liked that I shut up. That I never talked back. It didn't occur to me then that there are many ways to speak, and a voice is only one of them. After a while, I forgot I had ever said anything at all.

But silence, too, can dog you. My new friends would utter awful things about each other, would tell jokes that I reviled, and their words would bounce off my silence and come back to them as agreement. I began to feel like a quarry where people came to shout their ugly thoughts, to abandon them. I missed my voice, my echo—that bumbling, loyal mutt that would always stand up for me.

And so I moved back home, and I searched until at last I found my voice curled up, shivering and alone at the bottom of the quarry. It perked up at my approach, its timbre wagging with hesitant excitement, but it flinched when I reached out for it. I wanted to tell it how sorry I was, how it had done nothing wrong. But for the first time since abandoning it, even though my voice was right there in front of me, I felt truly speechless.

DIVING FOR PEARLS

I found a shoal of saltwater clams and dove into the swaying forest of kelp and brackish light to hunt for pearls.

I opened one and inside I found a warning not to compare myself to others.

In the next, an admonition not to focus on physical beauty.

The third told me not to be distracted by riches, for life's real treasure is knowledge.

I sighed and returned to the surface.

It wasn't that I didn't appreciate finding pearls of wisdom. But sometimes you're just looking for a nice pair of earrings for a Friday night.

THE MUSIC BOX: PART II

When my mother died, I finally went to visit my estranged sister.

"I need help destroying Mom's old music box," I told her.

"Why?"

"It's filled with the souls of one thousand and one tortured ghosts."

"What? Mom always told me it was one thousand."

I went quiet, and she gave me a puzzled look. Then she gasped and covered her mouth.

"You're not saying . . ."

I nodded.

"Mom."

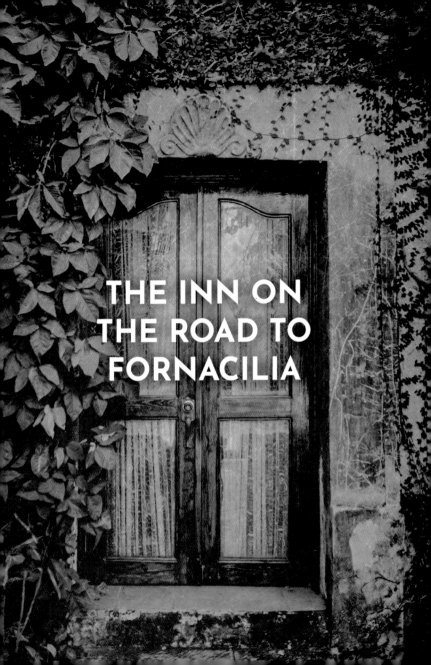

THE INN ON THE ROAD TO FORNACILIA

My traveling companion and I came to the inn at the crossroads in summer, intending to stay only a single night. We were wind-chilled and bone-weary, and while the road ahead at first seemed deserted, we rounded a bend to see the hearth light shimmering through broad cage windows. The concierge was standing in the doorway as if she were waiting for us. She did not ask how long we were staying, but whisked our bags up to rooms that had been prepared.

The next day, we awoke to find the sun high and the morning half gone. Determined to make up time, we descended to the common room for a quick breakfast and found many other late risers breaking their fast and chatting.

"I was on the road to Fornacilia when I found this place," said a retired sloop's captain. "I checked in for—well, I forget how long—but it's such a lovely place and I've never quite got around to leaving."

I made eye contact with my companion. He seemed eager to go. But the meal came, slow and leisurely, and by the time we were done, it was well into afternoon. We went up to our rooms to prepare for a half day on the road, but as storm clouds gathered outside, we thought better of it. One more night, then.

The next day, the concierge told us we couldn't leave without first taking a lunch in their famous vineyard. Still eager to be on the road, but charmed by the luxuries around us, we agreed to eat before heading out. But after roast partridge and a bottle of rosé spumante served on glacier ice, we found our heads thick and our wills weak. One more night, then.

And so we passed a languid week there—or maybe it was longer. The days were long and lazy, and the nights full of drink and dancing in the inn's courtyard. We would go to bed, bellies full and heads spinning, hearing voices in the corridor.

One morning, we saw newcomers speaking with the captain at breakfast.

"We were on our way to Gelsea when we saw this place and thought we'd stay for the night. How long have you been here?"

For a moment it seemed odd that I could not remember, odder still that the newcomers had found the inn on the road to one place, and the captain had found it on the road to another. My companion and I had been on our way to . . . we could no longer recall.

"We have to leave—tonight," he said. "We are all just prisoners here. I fear if we don't go now, we never will."

I meant to go with him, but that night the inn gathered for a feast, plating up a massive roast—some kind of meat I had not tasted before—and we gobbled up the beast with our wine-whetted appetites and steely knives. I have not seen my friend since, though sometimes his voice wakes me up in the middle of the night, as if he is calling from somewhere nearby.

My traveling companion and I came to the inn at the crossroads in summer—or perhaps I came alone. Or perhaps it was in autumn. The wine has gone to my head. It's winter now, at any rate, although the night man tells me you can find the staff here any time of year, whatever road you are on.

THE CRIMSON SINGERS

When we cross paths with one of the crimson singers, we unload every last bullet we have. We've survived long enough to see what a crimson singer can do to a man.

But when we cross paths with a full choir of them, well, we each save that last bullet for ourselves. We've survived long enough to see what a crimson singer can make a man do to himself.

THE BORED PIRATE ROBERTS

The Bored Pirate Roberts is spoken of in hushed tones about the islands.

When his sails, the color of old vellum, appear on the horizon, you know it is already too late. There is no escaping.

He'll board your vessel or land outside your town. "Tell us a story," he'll say.

And then he sits down cross-legged, and he won't leave until you do.

So we've been preparing. Over the years, we've ventured out to collect a fearsome arsenal of amusements: tall tales, short stories, old wives' tales, fables, follies, tragedies, comedies, romances, dusty books of ghost stories, myths, and anecdotes.

We see his sails on the horizon, and we are ready. He arrives in the harbor to find us lined up along the battlements: storytellers, elders, novelists, improvisers, actors, playwrights, shamans, bards, parents at bedtime, tavern gossipers, dramaturges, songwriters, and fibbers.

"Tell us a story," he says.

"No," we say. "*You* tell *us* a story."

And we sit down to listen.

Montrésor gripped his pen as sweat trickled from his brow and plopped onto the page. The ink bled into Rorschach blossoms, and a dark garden slowly grew out over the parchment. For a moment, he fancied he could see a shape emerging—a tree or a face—until it receded again into the obscure mass.

"Please, not again," he whispered as the candle stub burned low.

He looked down at the ink-soaked parchment, unable to remember what he'd written there, if anything. His sweat drops had made the letters swell and burst like angry blisters, filling the page with black. Should he begin again in white ink? His slender fingers trembled as they stroked the nib of his pen. He needed to write something, anything before the darkness came again.

"No! Not *anything*. Not that again!" he muttered.

The candle flickered indifferently. He knew there was not much time left. Outside, the wind and rain battered the window. The flame guttered, and terror clenched his hand around the pen. The darkness was almost here. Nowhere to go but downward, inward. He dipped the nib into his well of white ink and began to write furiously on the black page:

Montrésor gripped his pen as sweat trickled from his brow and plopped onto the page. The ink bled into Rorschach blossoms, and a dark garden slowly grew out over the parchment. For a moment, he fancied he could see a shape emerging—a tree or a face—until it receded again into the obscure mass . . .

THREE
WISHES

"I wish I was free," said the genie. Then he waited to see what would happen.

Admittedly, this loophole was questionable at best. The side of his lamp bore the engraved words, "Three wishes, but beware the price." However, it was forbidden for genies to grant their own wishes, so he'd tracked down a monkey's paw to wish upon. It curled its shriveled finger, signifying the granting of the wish.

The genie looked around to see if anything had changed.

Then he noticed the new engraving on his lamp.

"Free wishes, no consequences."

Well, shit.

The genie was free.

Just not for himself.

The colony had never encountered anything like the sleepstalkers. At first, we assumed they were nocturnal, hunting us when we're most likely to be unconscious. To keep safe, we switched to a daytime bunk schedule, but the attacks kept coming.

Next, we tried stimulants—the same ones the skeleton crew had used to keep alert during our long interstellar journey. We stayed up for days at a time, veins buzzing with coffee and amphetamines. But then the hallucinations started. Somehow, the sleepstalkers always knew to strike right as our minds wandered off.

Finally, we realized that the creatures don't hunt by light or sleep. They hunt by dreams, drawn to whatever waves our brains give off when they turn to fantasy. So our chemists studied how to dampen those signals, shutting down our ability to dream at all. And with that, the sleepstalkers began to starve.

Over the years they died out, and with them went a little piece of ourselves.

We'd set out with a dream to bring humanity to the farthest corners of the galaxy. By the time we got there, we'd left both dreams and humanity behind.

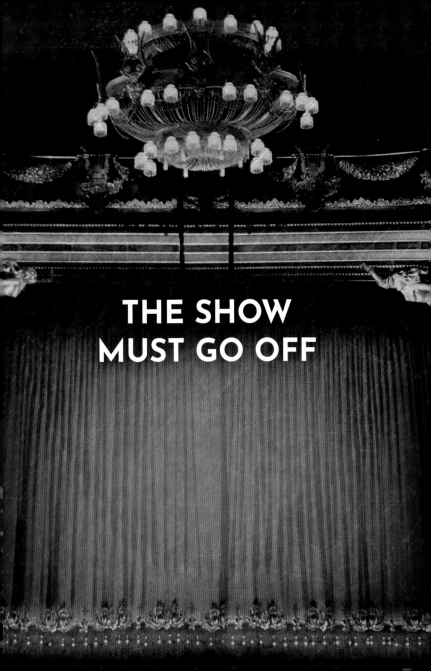

THE SHOW
MUST GO OFF

Andrea couldn't understand what had gone wrong. Her new musical had all the hallmarks of a smash hit success.

A sensational title.

A strong core cast of one dozen roles.

A controversial premise that would bring in the punters.

She thought people would beat down the doors to see the untold story of Jesus's twelve apostles and their elaborate plan to steal Jesus's body back from the tomb and stage his resurrection.

But alas, after a disastrous run of three days, it was curtains for *Jesus Heist Superstar.*

ELEKTROTRANSPORT "CII" ☎ 0937-24004

HIGH
GROUND

"It's a fungus, not a virus," Carey corrects me, shouting over the high wind.

The world is ending, and she cares about semantics. Still, it's the little things that kill you now. Inhale the yellow spores, and they spread to your brain. Then the urge hits. You need to get to high ground. You climb whatever you can find: trees, mountains, radio towers, office buildings.

"Hope we're high enough," she says, wiring the machine.

At first, I thought she was crazy to set up the suppressor on top of a skyscraper, but it makes sense to co-opt the fungus's strategy. It waits until you're elevated before it shuts down your brain. Shoots grow out from your nose, ears, and mouth and enclose your head in a mask of fungal blooms. The wind carries the spores to the next city. If Carey's machine works the way she says it will, she could stop the spread.

"Okay, hit the power," she says.

I'm about to flip the switch when I see it: the thin yellow tendril of fungus stretching out from her nostril. I hesitate.

"I'm fine, just start it."

"We should wait. You're sick."

"Start it," she insists in a voice not quite her own.

"No," I say. "Something's wrong. You're not all there."

"Not all there?" she says, stumbling over to hit the switch herself. The machine whirs to life and starts to spout a steady eruption of sickly yellow spores into the darkening sky.

"I am everywhere."

CROSSROADS
AT MIDNIGHT

I met the devil at the crossroads at midnight.

"Give me your soul and I will give you such wonderous stories to tell. Stories to astound men and women."

"But they wouldn't truly be mine. And I can already tell many stories that aren't mine."

"Then I will give you just one wonderous story that is yours alone."

"You already have," I said, walking away. Just wait until I tell my friends about this.

PULL DOWN
A STAR

"I would reach up into the night sky and pull down a star for you," he told her when they started dating.

Now, a few years into the relationship, she reminded him that he'd never quite got around to it. After a quick bit of searching, he found a website where you could gift a star for $20. It came with a certificate and everything.

The next day the star was delivered. A sad little thing, it cowered in its crate. It didn't come out until the delivery workers shook it out—none too gently.

"Careful," they said. "This one isn't house trained."

The company had misspelled his girlfriend's name on the certificate, but she was still delighted. She coaxed it over to her and cupped its shine in her hands. It let out a little nova of delighted kisses.

"Thank you," she said. "It's perfect."

The next few days were wonderful. Playing in the living room. Long walks in the park. It only took a few days of training to break the habit of the star leaking radiation on the living room floor.

But time wore on, and the couple's interest wore down. Its coloring began to change. The exuberant flare of the red giant faded into the silver maturity of a white dwarf, and suddenly there was no time for play or walks. The lawn was charred with countless rings of black and brown from all the times they let it out to dump its radiation.

"It's your turn," he'd say.

"It's always my turn," she'd reply.

"Yeah, well, it's your star."

Sometimes the star let off a solar flare in the living room, just for the attention. It could feel the love-hungry collapse of a black hole growing in its depths.

It had heard the boyfriend say he would reach up and pull down a star.

If only he was willing to reach down and pick up after one.

THE MUSIC BOX:
PART III

As the flames consumed our mother's music box, my sister and I felt its angry spirits shake the earth beneath our feet and thrash the branches above us. One thousand and one anguished souls evaporated into the night.

Then, at long last, the forest fell silent.

"Do you think the curse is over?" I asked.

My sister opened her mouth to speak, and out came the ghostly voices of boneless songbirds and an old widow's sobs.

"Close enough," I agreed.

THE STAG

"Please," said the stag, gasping. "Spare my life, and the forest will take mercy on you."

I had chased it to the end of a blind ravine. It looked a pitiful thing down the sights of my gun. Not an ounce of fat. Its skin and muscle were gnarled like blackened tree roots. It had been a long winter, and long winters breed bitter springs.

"I'm sorry," I said, taking aim, "but this is how I feed my children."

The spray of buckshot caved in its side like a boot striking a rotten log. Then one by one, the blood-slick pellets spilled out of the hollow in its flesh, dropping to the earth like wet, red seeds. Where they fell, gray-brown shoots began to sprout in the shape of antlers.

In the turf below my feet, I could feel fibrous bones growing, root cages twisting into skulls and spines, femurs and hooves. The soil churned as their skeletons reared from the black earth, antlers draped in nightworms and loam. They looked at me with hungry eyes. It had been a long winter, and long winters breed bitter springs.

"Please," I said, backing away, fumbling to reload.

"I'm sorry," said the stag, "but this is how I feed my children."

It lowered its antlers and charged.

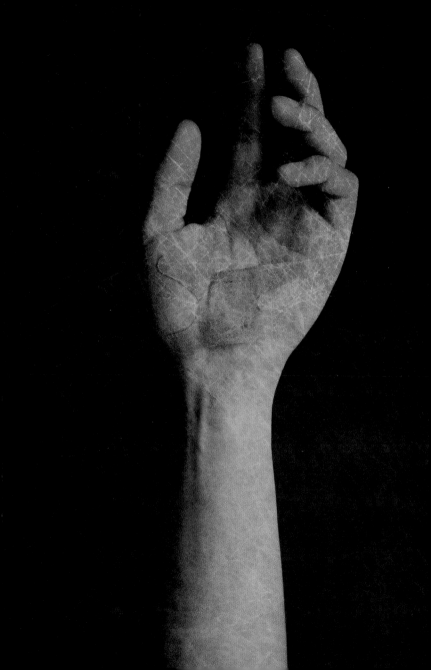

The camp medic assures me I don't have to tell the others about my bite. She says it's just a surface wound. Any symptoms I'm experiencing are unrelated. A seasonal bug, not the virus. Should clear up in a few days on its own.

So for a week, it's business as usual. Group supply runs. Sharing meals in the mess tent. Catching shut-eye in the bunkhouse when we can.

But as I get worse, I remember that the first symptoms of infection are false memories.

And our camp doesn't have a medic.

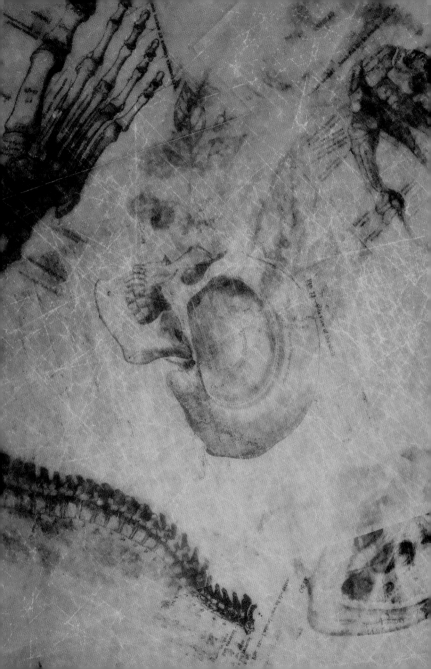

AN INFINITY
OF GHOSTS

Somewhere in the infinity of parallel universes, you are already dead: hit by a bus, fallen down the stairs, choked on a dinner roll, died in a gas leak, felled by an embolism.

And somewhere in the infinity of your parallel deaths, you came back as a ghost, tethered by the feeling that in some other life, things might have gone differently.

And somewhere in your infinity of parallel ghosts, your spirit is able to slip between dimensions, flipping the pages of another life like a visitor browsing a book in someone else's home.

And here you are now in the one reality you know, alive and reading these words, watched by an amphitheater of incredulous spirits from across space and time.

They are proud that you have come as far as you have in the book of life.

But even more than that, they are curious to see what happens when you turn the page.

NO.1   AMMUNITION HOIS

THE
GENERAL'S
BEARD

On the eve of battle, the soldiers whispered to one another about the general's new beard—a big, bushy, regal thing after only a week of growth.

The advance scouts claimed the general had vowed not to shave until he returned home victorious.

The rank and file speculated he was growing it to intimidate his enemies.

The officers thought it emphasized his command.

Over the flickering light of the campfire, the ragged troop could see the wounds this long and brutal campaign had carved into their bodies, into their minds, but they took heart knowing their great general had not cracked. They would rest easy and rise early, ready to face whatever fate would come.

Meanwhile, alone in his tent, the general sat and stared at his bushy face in the mirror, hand still shaking too much to shave.

THE DRAGON AND THE BARD

I, Jassa the Scribe, will record here in my own hand the quizzical encounter between the dragon and the bard.

The dragon had a hoard of gold he had collected as tribute from the surrounding villages over the years, and over which he was justly protective. He had been besieged by knights, assaulted by wizards, and stabbed by thieves. He thought he had seen everything the humans were willing to do for gold.

And then the bard walked into his hoard.

"Are you here to slay me?" asked the dragon.

"I'm here to sing," said the bard.

And sing she did. She sang of the wide world beyond the dragon's cave. She sang of great loves, of battles won and lost, of chance meetings and fateful partings. She sang of the great tapestry of life, of the threads of sorrow and joy that make up its fabric. She sang of how she dreamed to go and share her music with the world, that she might be part of the great tapestry and its endless weaving.

Moved to tears, the dragon bequeathed her a portion of his hoard so she could tour and perform before courts and campfires across the realm. He only asked that she return to him in a year's time to report on her adventures. She agreed and was faithful to her promise.

I, Jassa the Scribe, believe this event constitutes the first-ever application for public arts funding.

Furthermore, I beseech thee, o mighty dragon, for a stipend of gold that I might travel about the realm to collect further research for a new book on the influence of draconic patronage in the arts. I hear oral histories and interspecies relations are hot topics this year.

A GIRL
WHO'S GOT
EVERYTHING

The age-wizened mermaid glanced around her cavern of trinkets and treasures from the surface world. Despite her father's many warnings, she'd kept on collecting. Still, she couldn't help but notice how her haul had changed in recent years.

Instant coffee pods.

An empty tin of cat food.

A discarded soap bottle with a warning about "microplastic" contents.

Her father had always said not to trust the surface dwellers. Then he'd gotten caught in a trawler's net out by the great Pacific garbage patch and hauled away in a mass of panicked tuna. Glancing at the tin of cat food again, she sighed.

Perhaps he had been right after all.

THE
VANISHED
CONTINENT

I am not certain of much these days, but I am certain of this: ours was a great and powerful kingdom.

From our island, we ruled the seas and mapped the world and all its coastlines. So confident of our mastery were we that when we saw the mainland in the distance suddenly vanish from the coastline, we were in an uproar.

"It's a trick to get us to change our maps!" said the king's cartographer.

A day later the mainland seemed to reappear, but it blinked away again hours later.

"It's a trap to lure our ships out to investigate!" claimed the admiral.

Throughout the month, it continued to vanish and appear, like a fickle ghost on the shimmering horizon.

"It's an enchantment to hide their devious machinations from us!" claimed our seers.

To settle the matter, I was entrusted to make an investigatory expedition with a small crew. I was the obvious choice. I had returned safely from countless ocean voyages. But even I had an uneasy feeling as we set course for the silhouette of land that flickered in and out of our vision. Even when the wind died or the waves grew rough, our sloop carried on sailing as if carried by sheer force of will.

We drew near shore, and I spotted a fishing boat a few hundred yards out. A woman and her daughter sat together, oblivious to our approach.

"What's that island out there?" the girl asked, pointing to where we had come from. "I've never seen it before."

"We don't go there," her mother replied. "It's a ghost island. A long time ago, there was a very proud kingdom that thought it could conquer the sea. It was so proud that even after the water swallowed it whole, their island would still slip back into existence from time to time like an old memory. Every now and then someone claims to see a ghost ship sail out from its shores and then turn back just before landing on ours, but I don't hold with that nonsense."

Our ship passed within a few feet of theirs. They never looked up. I felt as if I was dissolving, burning up like sea fog in sunlight. I gave the crew orders to turn the ship around.

I am not certain of much these days, but I am certain of this: this is not the first time I have made the journey to find the vanished continent, nor will it be the last.

THE ECTO-
REACTOR

When the Ecto-Reactor was first installed, the government decided not to tell us we were drawing our electricity from the spirit world, a vortex of haunted souls and lingering regrets powerful enough to light up cities.

Sure, we had a vague sense of unease whenever we turned on the television or started the dishwasher, but that was nothing new. We had always known convenience had a price.

The government had done its job: keeping the lights of civilization burning.

And we did ours: ignoring the screams coming from the wires in the walls.

THE BONES
BENEATH

"I'd be useless in a zombie apocalypse," you once joked to me over a cup of tea in my living room. "I'm too softhearted."

And yet when the world came undone—when the lights went dark and food ran low and the knives came out—we needed you. For all the apocalypse fantasies we had nursed of being strong and resourceful and independent, we needed you more than we'd ever admit.

The more the world unravels, the more it needs people who feel and listen, who wipe away tears and open the saferoom door for one more lost soul when the rest of us would shut it and call our fear "strength."

It needs people who tell stories and dream of a tomorrow not grimed over with the mud and sweat of today, who help us bury our dead and plunge our hands deep into the pools of our grief when the blood on them gets to be too much.

It needs people who remind us that what keeps us moving is not some kind of unholy shambling grudge against death, but an unholy shambling love, a belief that when the skin of the world has been ripped away and we are left to stare at the bones beneath, we can still gather around the campfire, brew a cup of tea, and talk.

THE ANGER
THIEF

The anger thief steals people's ire before it can swelter into full-blown rage. Soft-shoed and nimble-fingered, he weaves his way through long checkout lines, crowded emergency rooms, comment threads, snowbound airports, and stranded buses, plucking frustration as it ripens.

People speculate about what he does with it all. Perhaps he's stockpiling for a day of furious reckoning. Perhaps he keeps it in a lead-lined vault marked "radioactive," hoping it will never be unleashed on the world.

I choose to believe he slips it back into our pockets when we need it most: the conviction to speak up for ourselves, to stand up for others, act boldly for the greater good.

Perhaps he's not a thief at all, but a Robin Hood, redistributing anger like the gold of greedy kings. None of us wants to think that our outrage is anything other than our divine right, the justice of an aggrieved universe shining through us. It would make us angry to know our rage bears the same weight and value as anyone else's.

And heaven knows there's enough anger going around already.

SICK DAYS

The interrovirus spread across the planet in days,
forcing us to speak only in questions.
　　"Have you heard?"
　　"How are you?"
　　"What's wrong?"
　　"Can I help?"

For many of us, it's a reprieve. We feel like we're finally listening instead of waiting for our turn to talk.

Today, I finished developing a cure, but I've decided to sit on it a while longer.

The world could use a few more sick days.

ELEMENTALS

After the sick ward filled with students exhibiting the same strange burns and poisoning symptoms, the College of Mages held an emergency meeting in the Hall of the Elements.

"When we granted each initiate permission to summon the elemental of their choice," said the headmaster, "we assumed you would wield your power responsibly."

The fire initiates nodded in furious agreement.

The earth initiates listened patiently.

The air initiates sighed in assent.

The water initiates bobbed their heads, calm as a windless pond.

At the back of the hall, Carl the science initiate looked at his plutonium elemental and began to sweat nervously.

AUNT ELLEN'S
DOLL
COLLECTION

As children, we hated staying at Aunt Ellen's house when our parents went out of town.

My sister and I were convinced her collection of antique dolls in the guest bedroom was alive, that at any moment one could escape the massive glass display cabinet and attack. We were terrified of waking up during the night to find one less doll on the shelf and a porcelain face watching from somewhere in the dark.

"Nonsense," Aunt Ellen chided us. "The dolls can't escape."

She was telling the truth of course.

When I woke up to find my sister trapped inside the cabinet, no amount of hammering could break her out.

And as her body shrank and her terrified face smoothed to porcelain, I realized the danger had never been finding one less doll on those shelves.

It was finding one more.

THE HANGING
OF DOCTOR
ELISE TREBIA

When they shut down Dr. Trebia's laboratory, the headlines were something out of a penny dreadful: human experimentation, forcible imprisonment, bodysnatching, mistreatment of corpses.

The trial was a spectacle, and the papers served every detail to a hungry public. Trebia denied nothing. Her solicitor fought tooth and nail, but the doctor was too proud of her grisly work to cooperate. With her contemptuous smirk on the witness stand, she seemed unafraid to die for her crimes.

The sentence came down like a hammer. In the interest of public decency, the court burned her research and pronounced the good doctor would go to the gallows in a year's time. She conferred with her counsel, but filed no appeals. She only asked for a rudimentary chemistry set to while away time in her holding cell and a private meeting with her solicitor on the day of her death. The court assented.

On the morning of the execution, a crowd gathered to watch. No one had expected the doctor's resolve to break after so long, but break it did. Gone was the smirk.

"Stop! It wasn't me!" she screamed as they dragged her out. She turned to her solicitor. "What have you done? They're going to kill me!"

The meeting hadn't gone well, apparently. The solicitor shook his head sadly. He had only come to have a final drink with his client in private, just as she'd requested. Perhaps she'd been hoping he'd save her. One final appeal. One last trick to escape the hangman. How else to explain her cracking after a year of silence?

And so the hangman fitted the noose, and after a brief dance, the good doctor was silent again.

The papers recounted the particulars of the day with great relish, but there was one detail they missed. If someone had been watching closely, they might have seen her solicitor's smirk as the hangman pulled the trapdoor lever, familiar to anyone who had attended the doctor's trial.

And perhaps if the court hadn't destroyed Dr. Trebia's files, they might have known what she was researching: the transfer of consciousness from one body to another via chemical means. They might have even seen how close she was to a breakthrough.

But the doctor was dead and buried now, and her papers were ash on the wind.

As for her solicitor, the whole ordeal had seemingly convinced him to take a year away from the law to pursue other interests. Perhaps he'd try his hand at chemistry. He had just inherited a set, after all. And it was amazing what a brilliant mind could achieve with the right equipment and a year of time.

DEADRUNNERS

The Deadrunners were the most infamous pizza delivery service in Hustle City.

At the start of every delivery, they drank a heart-stopping poison. They didn't receive the antidote until they handed over the food.

Their pizzas were never cold on arrival.
If only the same could be said for the delivery boys.

When I retired, I realized I had wasted my life. I hadn't achieved anything I'd promised myself I would do when I settled for a life of water cooler chat and Mondays. I'd never finished my science degree. Never had a family of my own. Never started my inventor's workshop. Never invented anything.

So I did what any rational person would do: I resolved to build a time machine. I would go back and reclaim my life for loftier goals.

Progress was slow. As I tinkered, I started taking refresher science courses at the local college. The reading was difficult, and my fellow students found the septuagenarian in their midst to be a novelty.

"Why start school now?" they asked.

"I'm building a time machine," I told them.

First they laughed. Then they asked to see it. My little bungalow was too small to host everyone, so we moved my workshop into an empty dorm floor on campus. Students would drop in to see what I was doing, debate the design, and then return hours later with new components and ideas.

The work gradually progressed, and as my new friends graduated, some became professors and advised on the project. Others joined me full time. Floor by floor, our project took over the dorm.

It took twenty years, but we finally think we have something. The whole campus is involved now, and we decide to make a day of the unveiling. We wheel the machine into the quad, where a crowd has gathered. Former classmates have come from around the country to see.

Sadly, things don't go as planned. When I pull the lever, the machine sucks all the power from the city grid, but still won't start. Perhaps if we build a dedicated reactor? My friends begin making sketches. With another fifteen to twenty years, surely it will work. I sigh. I am ninety-five. I don't have that much time.

I look around at those who have gathered: at the dean who last year gave me my honorary degree; at the community of dreamers who took me in; at my inventor's workshop, which is expanding to a second building in the spring. No one looks disappointed. They are excited. I suppose I am too.

This machine has transported us through twenty years of divergent lives to stand together in the same moment. It has given me the life I thought I wasted: my degree, my family, my workshop.

So what if it doesn't work?

LIFE
EVERLASTING

He didn't become a lich to obtain life everlasting. He just didn't want to die like the rest of his generation: gone in their twenties from disease, famine, drought, war, or malnutrition. Fifty years more. That was all he asked.

He tried potions and spells. He ransacked books and scrolls. Finally, he found the ritual he was looking for. It would put him into a deep slumber, and for every ten years he stayed sleeping, his waking life would be extended by one year. He would awake to find the world he knew changed beyond recognition. Gone would be everything familiar. He would even forget his own name. It was a terrible price, but he was willing to pay.

So he found a tomb to lay in, and he slept a dreamless sleep for five hundred years as, outside, everything he knew crumbled to dust and passed from memory.

When he awoke, a newly minted lich, he prepared himself to emerge from the darkness into the glory of his newfound longevity. This was the moment he had sacrificed everything for. He had given up his family, his humanity, even his name—all to stave off death a little longer.

He left the tomb to find that the world had moved on without him. Socialized medicine and ample food meant that most people lived to eighty, sometimes even one hundred.

And so he went back to his tomb to sulk. Perhaps he'd try again in another five hundred years.

"When you walk in the woods of the Briar Goddess, keep to the path," the town elder warned me from his sickbed. "She demands a soul for every plant taken from her great garden, but she cannot touch you if you keep to the path. She will do anything, pull any trick, to ensure her price is paid."

I nodded. I had been dreading this journey for days. My younger brother had offered to go in my place, but after I caught him meeting with the elder, I had forbidden it. The elder, who had led our town for as long as anyone could remember, was getting worse. The only thing that could heal him now was Dead Man's Wish, the herb that grows in the heart of the forest.

I bid my brother goodbye and set out at a careful pace, sticking to the path. After an hour, I heard a voice calling from deep in the tangled green.

"Help! Help! I'm stuck!"

It was my brother's voice. I wanted to plunge into the thickets to find him, but I recalled the elder's warning.

"Cry all you want, woods witch," I said. "I must keep to the path."

I walked on, but as I ventured deeper, my brother's screams grew desperate.

"Please, brother! The elder said you'd lost your way and sent me to find you!"

"That's not him," I said to myself. "I must keep to the path."

Finally, I reached a clearing where I could see Dead Man's Wish growing like bony fingers from the loam.

"If you take from my garden," warned a voice from the edge of the clearing, "the price *will* be paid, one way or another."

I looked up to see the goddess, her body woven from twisted vines and grasping brambles. Her eyes were two rotting berries, her hair a mass of beetles. She held my brother by the arm, or some illusion that looked just like him, right down to the fear in his eyes.

"It's a trick," I said. "The elder warned me you would say anything to get what you want."

"And do you not think he would do the same?" she replied.

I tried to keep her words from my mind as I stepped forward and picked the herb. She watched as I backed away, keeping her in my eyeline.

"Later you will remember my words and know I tried to warn you," she said.

All I could do was repeat my mantra. *Keep to the path. Keep to the path.*

I returned in time to save our elder. He thanked me with a sad look in his eyes.

"It's your brother," he said. "He wandered into the woods after you. He never came back."

And as our town celebrates the good health of our leader, I wonder if that was my brother I saw out there in the briar. I wonder about the fear in his eyes. I have looked in the elder's books of herb lore and seen that Dead Man's Wish does not cure illness. It extends life past its natural boundaries. It is customary to send two boys to gather it, knowing only one will live to carry it back. And there were two of us out in those woods.

But, no, I mustn't wonder. The elder has guided us throughout his long, long life. Surely he wouldn't lead us astray now. And anyhow, I made my choice. I must keep to the path.

THE VINES OF
SORREASTRO

The vines of Sorreastro present themselves only to those whom Fortune has spurned and Despair has courted: perhaps a ruined farmer, or a bankrupt vintner, or a gourmand who feels they have lived too long. You will be making your way to the sea to hurl yourself in when you see it—an overgrown vineyard twisting with vines and bursting with grapes the color of a rose-gold sunset. Some have found it as far north as Boreona, or as far south as Cape Coronet, but you have found it here, in the place where you decided to end your life.

And for a moment, your curiosity is equal to your despair. For you want to know who would let such a beautiful vineyard go to shambles. It is enough to draw you away from the cliffs for a few paces. After all, it is early in the day and you have no more appointments to keep.

You climb to the vines to find they are near harvest. A crumbling farmhouse sits amongst the leaves, untended for years. Walking through the collapsed door, you dig through the cupboards, trying to understand who would abandon this place, but there is nothing to tell you. And as you sort the clutter, you find yourself arranging things as you would have organized them. You sweep and wipe and tidy up. Before long, the kitchen looks almost habitable again. And perhaps you could stay—just for a day. You are in no rush, and the grapes outside will need to be gathered or they will rot on the vine.

The work goes well, but you will need a few more days to gather all the fruit. Perhaps a week. Luckily there is a spring nearby to fuel your thirsty work, and grapes enough to eat, and still more to make into wine. You have everything you need here.

And by the time you are done, the season is gone, and you have decided to stay until spring. And perhaps you will stay the winter, or perhaps you will hurl yourself into the sea. Perhaps you will stay another ten years, or perhaps you left this place the day you arrived. Everyone leaves Sorreastro differently, but for many, there is a moment when they feel that someone else will need this place, and it is time to let the vines reclaim it.

We don't know where you will go when you leave. Perhaps you'll return to your appointment with the sea. Perhaps you'll go back to the world that once spurned you. Some have said Sorreastro is merely a consolation stop for those at the end of their road. Others say it is the point where they are reminded they can always turn back. And please do remember you can always turn back.

Whatever you decide out there, far from the chatter of the world, know this: you may not see a vineyard or a crumbling farmhouse from where you are standing, but if you give yourself a moment to look around, there where the earth falls away and the waves crash, you might find Sorreastro, a moment of peace, and a ruin in need of a keeper.

I still remember the first time I adopted a home. When I entered the old house at 136 Prewitt Lane, it bristled with anger, letting me know I was not welcome. (As it had done for the past five would-be tenants.)

The walls began to shake, the lights flickering and buzzing, flakes of ancient paint falling from the ceiling like dead petals from a flower.

"There, there," I said, stroking the doorframe. "No need for that."

The shaking subsided, but I could feel distrust simmering behind the walls.

"Look," I said. "I won't stay long. Just a few minutes reading my book."

I could feel it watching me, confused, as I sat down in a dusty armchair. This is how you have to do it with the really traumatized houses. Get them used to human contact, a bit at a time. As expected, the cheeky thing acted out before I left. The soot of the fireplace coalesced into a grasping hand.

"None of that," I said in a voice that was firm, but loving. "I know you're hurt and scared, but you can relax. I'm here to help." I made a point of finishing my chapter before I stood. "I'll come back the same time tomorrow."

The next visit went better. It still rattled the chandeliers when I showed up, but halfheartedly. It let me read two chapters before it tried to spook me with the sound of fingernails scratching behind the walls. I just stroked the carpet gently until it calmed down. Its distrust was turning to curiosity. It had seen so many people leave, but it had never seen one come back.

After a week of visits, it let me stay the night. By the next month, a string of overnights had become a week. It let me mop its old oak floorboards, vacuum the carpets, and scrub off the flaking paint to apply a new coat. It still shook, but it seemed to be from enjoyment—the kicking leg of an itch scratched.

I've heard it said that some houses are evil, but I disagree. They just miss their old owners, or they feel abandoned, and so they lash out. Their misbehavior drives people away, and over time they forget how it feels to be loved. When you foster homes like I do, your job is to help them remember. It's not so hard.

So please, come in—oh, but take off your boots. This one is still a little nervous around people in shoes. Still not quite sure why, though I have some guesses.

If you adopt, there are a few quirks you'll have to get used to, but you'll learn to love them. Yes, the faucets still sometimes scream when you turn them, and you'll have to mop the occasional puddle of blood that appears overnight, but it's made such progress.

I think it's finally ready to be a forever home again.

A FAREWELL

This is not goodbye, because you are not leaving. Not really. You can never really leave a place like The House of Untold Stories. Years from now, you will still find its traces on you, the way you find the fur of a passed-on pet stuck to an old coat or caught in the gap of a loose baseboard.

This is not goodbye, because you will be back. Or you will remember how it felt to stand here, on the threshold of memory and fantasy, and you will return to the dance of dust motes in slanted sunlight, to a childhood home made unfamiliar by emptiness, to the dim cupboard where you keep the thoughts you only sometimes use.

This is not goodbye, because you carry the House with you. You could map it in the swinging doors and hidden hallways of your mind, something secret you contain within the walls of yourself the way the House has contained you here.

This is not goodbye, but it is time to go. The world is waiting, the way the world always has. Courage, my friend. Place your hand on the latch. Turn the page. And when the door clicks shut, remember to come back soon.